CALUM'S CUP FINAL

For Fraser, Thomas, Graeme and Freya – D.S.

To my mum for being the nicest person I've ever met.
I've been so lucky to have such great parents
– and grandparents for my children – A.A.M.

Young Kelpies is an imprint of Floris Books
First published in 2016 by Floris Books

Text © 2016 Danny Scott. Illustrations © 2016 Floris Books
Danny Scott and Alice A. Morentorn have asserted their rights
under the Copyright, Designs and Patent Act 1988 to
be identified as the Author and Illustrator of this work

The publisher acknowledges subsidy from
Creative Scotland towards the publication
of this volume

MIX
Paper from
responsible sources
FSC® C007785
www.fsc.org

This book is also
available as an eBook

British Library CIP data available
ISBN 978-178250-282-1
Printed in Great Britain by Bell & Bain ltd

CALUM'S CUP FINAL

written by **Danny Scott**

illustrated by **Alice A. Morentorn**

Young
Kelpies

CALUM FERGUSON

ERIKA BROWN

FRASER MCDONALD

LEO NKWANU

JANEK POWOLSKI

NOAH HAMPTON

RAVI GUPTA

JORDAN MCPRIDE

The Final Training Session

Caleytown Primary after-school club was enjoying the sight of their famous P6 footballers cleaning up the playground.

The team did their best to ignore the taunts coming from inside the school.

The team's coach, Mr McKlop, was oblivious to it all. He held open a giant black bin bag and shouted instructions.

"Remember, lads, one piece of litter at a

time, and you *must* keep control of the ball until you've put the litter in the bag. If you lose control, go back to where you started."

"Any ideas why we're doing this instead of playing football, Cal?" whispered Calum's best friend Leo.

"I dunno," Calum replied, plucking a wet crisp packet from a branch, football under his foot. "But anything's better than sitting about, worrying about the tournament."

"Are you worried? I can't wait to play at Heroes Glen!"

Leo's confidence surprised Calum. He'd just assumed everyone else was as nervous as he was. As Calum dribbled back to Mr McKlop's

bin bag, holding on to the soggy packet,
he didn't notice Lewis Budge dribbling straight
for him...

Lewis and Calum bounced off each other and landed on their bums. The after-school club's howls of delight echoed out the window.

"Your litter's blowing away, Calum," said Mr McKlop before Lewis or Calum could speak.

Calum watched the wind carry his crisp packet back across the playground. He pushed himself up again and dribbled after it.

"Watch where you're going next time, buddy," Lewis muttered behind him.

A few minutes later, satisfied with the state of the playground at last, Mr McKlop blew his whistle. He zipped up his tracksuit, packed the balls away and led the team out for a quick jog through Caleytown. His thick brown hair flopped up and down with each step.

"Fall in behind me, gentlemen!"

The squad filtered out through the gates and jogged past Caleytown's mixture of old and new houses. They eventually came to a stop outside Mr Aziz's corner shop, Calum's favourite hang-out.

In the window, Mr Aziz had put up a poster. It showed their team picture from a recent playoff win against local rivals Muckleton Primary. Calum picked out his grinning, freckled face, and cringed.

The door's chime rang and Mr Aziz stepped out to greet them. He beamed at the squad. "Aha, it's the pride of Caleytown! Mr McKlop tells me you'd like to help me unload my van?"

The players looked at each other. This was news to them.

"Do we get free chocolate for this?" Jordan asked.

Mr McKlop gave him a stern look and clapped his hands together. "Let's get to it."

The narrow aisles in Mr Aziz's shop became like a busy car park, with players trying to squeeze past each other as they ferried boxes from van to storeroom. Progress was especially hard for the show offs like Ravi and Jordan who

were trying to carry three boxes at a time.

We should form a chain, Calum thought to himself. He didn't dare speak up in case Jordan, Ravi and Lewis made fun of him.

After the fourth or fifth collision, team captain Janek let out a loud whistle. "Let's form a chain, Caleytown!"

Calum nodded his agreement. Having Janek around really did lift the pressure off everyone else.

"Good thinking, gents," said Mr McKlop. He watched the boxes fly along the chain. "Once we're done here, it's back to school to clean the minibus."

"For goodness' sake," Lewis muttered.

"What was that, Mr Budge?" Mr McKlop adjusted his glasses.

"I said, 'That sounds great, sir.'"
Lewis crunched his freckles up into a smile.

"Good. Trust me, you'll feel the benefit of this training when you get to Heroes Glen."

Skeerunch

It was the morning of the Scotland Stars National Soccer Sevens Tournament.

Loud rock music blared out of the minibus stereo. Coach Brown, the American coach of Caleytown Primary's girls' team, was driving the team to Heroes Glen Indoor Arena, where they would meet Mr McKlop. She was banging her head in time with the beat and singing along.

Next to her in the front seat sat Erika, the boys' team's reserve goalkeeper and

Coach Brown's daughter. The Browns lived next door to Calum's family, and Erika and Calum often played football together in their back gardens. Erika had the same bushy ponytail as her mum, but a very different taste in music – which is why she had her earphones in.

Leo cleared his throat to shout over the din. "We're in Group B with three other teams." He glanced down at the tournament programme. "And the winners of each group will play for the cup."

GROUP A	GROUP B
Portstruther Primary Fife Fighters League Champions	Caleytown Primary Central Wildcats League Champions
Royal Road Primary Glasgow Steelers League Champions	Fairydean Primary Border Bandits League Champions
Tayport Primary Dundee Dragons League Champions	Scapa Primary Highland Warriors League Champions
Forth Hill Primary Edinburgh Knights League Champions	Tewel Primary Aberdeen Wolverines League Champions

"What does it say about the teams in our group?" Fraser peered over Leo's shoulder.

"Not much." Leo moved to block Fraser's view. "Scapa are a hard-running team, Tewel sound... well, a lot like us. There isn't much info about Fairydean."

"What does it say about Royal Road?" Ravi shouted. He was busy up the back of the bus using his phone's screen as a mirror to check on his large quiff.

"Who are Royal Road?" Calum shouted back.

"What? You mean, you haven't heard of *Royal Road*?" Fraser turned his huge, cartoon-like eyes to Calum.

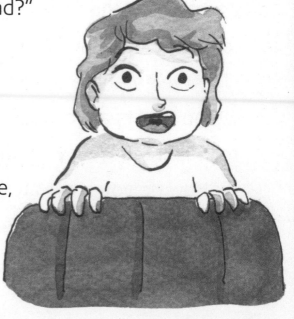

"How have you not heard of *Royal Road*?!" Leo gasped in mock astonishment.

Max, Ryan and Jordan looked at each other, amazed. It was clear that Calum was the only person who knew nothing about this team.

Fraser took a deep breath. "Royal Road are meant to be the best P6 football team in the country. And the richest." He looked from face to face. They all nodded for him to carry on. "They've got three coaches, branded strips, all the latest gadgets – they even went to Spain to prepare for today's tournament."

"How do you know all this inside info, Frazz?" Jordan raised an eyebrow.

"Well," said Fraser, "all Royal Road's trips, coaches and gear are paid for by my mum's boss Proctor Hampton."

SKEEEEEEERunCH

At first Calum wasn't sure if the grinding noise came from his nervous stomach or the minibus – until Coach Brown swung over to the side of the road and switched off the music.

"Bad news, boys. This piece of junk's finally given up. We'll have to walk the rest of the way – it's not too far."

"Fine by me." A travel-sick Lewis barged his way off the minibus.

"Umm, the rest of you fellas are gonna have to help carry some stuff." Coach Brown pointed towards the back of the minibus, where the bag of balls, the water bottles and the kitbag were stored. She looked at her watch. "And make it snappy."

Caleytown emerged from the minibus, blinking into the hot May sunshine. In the distance, Heroes Glen Indoor Arena shimmered like a palace in a concrete desert.

"Could you help me with this, please, Calum?" Janek tapped Calum on the shoulder. He was struggling with the big kitbag full of strips.

"Sure." Calum grabbed one of the bag's handles.

"Alrighty. Let's go!" Coach Brown pulled her baseball cap on and led the way.

3

Scotland Stars TV

Scotland's never this hot. What's wrong with today?!

My arms are on fire.

I'm going to be too knackered to play!

The sun beat down on the team as they heaved their kit and supplies across Heroes Glen's vast car park. Most of the players had taken their tops off and tied them around their waists.

Lewis had his tied round his head to stop his pale skin from burning.

Calum glanced sideways at Janek. The captain's ice-blue eyes were staring straight ahead.

"Are you nervous about today, Janek?"

"No," Janek replied. Caleytown's captain wasn't much of a talker.

"I'm kind of dreading it," Calum admitted.

"Then why play?" asked Janek.

"I... I'm sure I'll enjoy it if we win..." Calum was saying, when the kitbag handle was suddenly lifted from his hand.

"I'll take this, gentlemen. We need you two fresh for today!" Mr McKlop winked.

Calum smiled up at his teacher and coach. He looked smart in a dark blue suit.

"Nice threads, Mr McKlop!" said Ravi.

"Er, thanks, Mr Gupta," replied Mr McKlop. He turned to Coach Brown. "I take it the old minibus finally gave up the ghost?"

"Sure did," Coach Brown said.

"It's never straightforward with Caleytown,

is it?" Mr McKlop shook his head. "Onwards, team."

The team set off for the entrance with a fresh bounce in their step. As they neared the bustling entrance to Heroes Glen Jordan and Ravi quickened their pace.

"Make yourself look good, boys!" Jordan McPride shouted. He popped up his collar. "You're about to be on Scotland Stars TV."

Staring back at them was a camera crew and Scotland Stars' reporter Reiss Robertson. He wheeled up to them with a microphone in his lap.

"Caleytown Primary, right?" said Reiss Robertson. "Welcome to Heroes Glen! Er, you do realise your bus driver could have dropped you off at the entrance?"

Caleytown's players stared at him like he'd just told them how to pour a glass of water.

"*Ok*, anyway, we're just doing some interviews for the Scotland Stars website," Reiss continued. "Why don't you each take turns to tell the camera your name and position, starting with... you – you with the collar up."

While his teammates tidied themselves up as much as they could after their walk from the minibus, Jordan cleared his throat and looked straight at the camera.

"The name's McPride, Jordan McPride, defender and vice captain."

"You're not vice captain, Jordan," Leo said. "We don't even have a vice captain."

"Whatever, Leo." Jordan received a series of fist bumps from Ravi, Ryan and Lewis.

Reiss Robertson waved Leo forward to do his introduction.

"I'm Leo Nkwanu and you *will not catch me* on the left wing." Leo high-fived Fraser before pushing Calum forward.

"Hello, ahem, I am, ahem, Calum Ferguson..."
Calum could feel the sun beating down on his
straw-like hair. "If selected, ahem, I will wear
number nine and play striker. Thanks, bye."

He could hear Jordan, Lewis and Ravi
laughing into their hands. Calum cringed as all
his other teammates introduced themselves
with confidence.

"Thanks Caleyto—" Reiss Robertson's
attention was suddenly seized by a shiny silver
bus that was purring towards the entrance.

It came to a stop with a satisfied sigh, and
there was a brief pause before player after
player dropped down onto the tarmac. They
were all wearing white tracksuits with golden

trim and their initials sewn on the chest.

"Royal Road," Fraser whispered in awe.

"Are they even the same age as us?"
Leo said. "They look about fifteen!"

The panels on the side of the bus lifted into the air, revealing piles of branded kitbags and footballs in the luggage compartments.

A picture of cool, the Royal Road players stood and stared at Caleytown.

Janek moved to the front of the group to stare back.

"Ahem." Reiss Robertson cleared his throat. It was Caleytown's cue to make way, on his temporary stage, for Royal Road.

Heroes Glen
Indoor Arena

Inside, Heroes Glen was like an aircraft hangar. Along the curved roof long rows of lights stretched the length of the building like manmade stars.

"Whoa, this is... whoa..." Jordan summed up what his teammates were thinking.

The team stood on a shiny concrete concourse overlooking a full-sized indoor pitch. In front of them, several rows of seating formed steps down to the dugouts on the sideline. Scotland Stars banners were hanging all around them, as well as individual banners for each school team.

Goals with crisp, white nets were already laid out on two separate pitches for their seven-a-side matches.

"Can we go check it out, Mr McKlop? Coach Brown?" Leo asked, grabbing a football from the ball bag.

"Ok, but stay out of mischief. Coach Brown and I can see you from up here, remember."

The squad hurried down the steps to the pitch while their coaches headed for the registration desk.

"Look!" Calum pointed to an area marked 'Media Zone', where a cluster of kids and adults in Scotland Stars polo shirts were tapping away on tablets and computers.

"No pressure, aye?" Leo winked at Calum, whose stomach felt like a shaken can of fizzy juice.

On the pitch it was nice and cool. Several grown-ups wearing suits and tracksuits were standing around chatting to each other. Calum spotted the badges and colours of some famous Scottish and English clubs on their chests.

"They must be scouts," Leo whispered, bouncing on the balls of his feet. "Hey, this Astroturf is just like grass."

Calum nodded. *Maybe a run about will help me relax.*

"I'll bet I can hit the roof with a kick," Jordan said, desperate for an opportunity to show off in front of the scouts.

Calum looked up. From high on the ceiling, the people on the pitch below must have looked like little boats in a sea of green.

"I'll bet you can't," Leo said.

"This isn't a great idea, Jordan," Erika said, looking up to the concourse to check if her mum was watching them.

"Go on, Jordi. Give it a go," Ravi said, nodding his quiff back and forth in encouragement.

It was all the encouragement Jordan needed. He grabbed the football, lined up his kick and hoofed the ball into the air. His punt rose up and sideways. It soared nowhere near the roof but was right on course to land on the scouts.

"HEADS!" Jordan shouted. Everyone ducked. Luckily for him, his kick didn't hit anyone but landed right in the middle of a group of adults. They jumped back, sending jets of coffee into the air.

"What the..." One of younger men spun round to look at them.

"It's James Cauldfield," Calum and Leo gasped together as they recognised their favourite player from their favourite team, King's Park Athletic. He was an ex-pupil of their school and had come to watch them play earlier in the season.

"Caleytown Primary, I might have known." James Cauldfield shook his head. Next to him was a man with red curly hair and hard, blue eyes. He fixed the team with a terrifying stare, while shaking the hot coffee off his hand.

Caleytown were speechless. The angry man was none other than Scotland manager Graeme

Fletcher. He was taller in real life than on television, and much scarier.

The sound of Mr McKlop's footfall broke Fletcher's hard stare.

"I'm so sorry, Mr Fletcher, Mr Cauldfield," Mr McKlop panted as he arrived. "Can't turn your back for a second, and all that."

"Don't worry." James Cauldfield waved. "I'll calm the gaffer down."

Graeme Fletcher still did not look amused.

Jordan cleared his throat. "Hi, Mr Fletcher. I don't know if you recognise me but my dad, Andrew McPride, used to play for King's Park Athletic..."

"Oh boy, here we go," Leo muttered, but Mr McKlop intervened on everyone's behalf.

"Let's leave Mr Fletcher to his meeting, Jordan. You lot, this way. Now." Mr McKlop pointed his squad towards a sign that said:

CHANGING ROOMS AND PITCH TWO

"There's another pitch?" Fraser said, with even wider eyes than normal.

"Aye. It's where you lot can get warmed up, out of harm's way," Mr McKlop replied.

"I remember Andrew McPride," Graeme Fletcher called after them, rolling each 'r'.

Jordan spun round.

"He was quite the player. *He* could have hit the roof with a kick." Graeme Fletcher smiled in the way other people grimaced.

"Ha!" Jordan said, it was clear that he wasn't sure whether to gloat or cry.

Dodgeball

Calum, in a fluorescent bib, zipped into space near Erika's goal and called for the ball.

Fraser back-heeled it to him.

On the other team, Janek ran over to block Calum's path.

Not for the first time, Calum realised how hard it must be for other teams to come up against their captain in defence.

"Remember, lads, only two touches allowed," Mr McKlop shouted.

Calum had already taken a touch to control Fraser's pass and decided, in an instant, to shoot. His quick toe-poke snuck past Janek, caught Erika off guard and glanced in off the post. She wasn't happy: she and Calum had a long rivalry based on the hours they'd spent in his back garden practising penalties.

"Nice finish, Calum," Janek said, hands on hips.

"Thanks." Calum nodded. Toe-pokes were never a cause for celebration, but Janek didn't give out compliments very often.

Over on the sideline, Royal Road's players started to gather like clouds, in their pristine white tracksuits. Their coaching team started pointing things out to the squad about

Caleytown's players. One of them was even holding up a tablet and filming their warm-up.

"That must be Noah Hampton." Fraser nodded towards a boy with amber eyes who had 'NH' sewn on his tracksuit. He was tall, tanned and stood with his chest thrust out. "Standing next to his dad, Proctor Hampton."

Calum didn't like being watched by Royal Road. "What should we do?"

"Ignore them," Leo interrupted, desperate to get on with the warm-up.

But Calum couldn't

ignore all those eyes on him. When the game restarted he jogged forward and hid behind Janek.

On the other team, Leo wasn't intimidated. He made the most of his two touches to combine with Lewis in a series of one-twos, before belting the ball past Ravi.

A second Royal Road coach raised his tablet into the air to start filming Leo.

Coach Brown had seen enough.

"Excuse me, do y'all mind?" She stormed across the makeshift pitch, her ponytail swinging in her wake. "You're putting my players off their warm-up."

The Royal Road coaches just stood there,

mutely staring at her as if she were an animal at the zoo. Mr McKlop and his players quickly formed a half-circle behind her.

"I don't remember us giving you permission to film our warm-up," Mr McKlop added.

After an awkward pause, each of Royal Road's three coaches, plus Proctor Hampton, moved off to their own warm-up area.

Noah Hampton lingered behind. "Thanks for turning up to *our* tournament, Caleyville."

"Caley*TOWN*," Leo fired back. "Go and read the trophy if you need a reminder. Our name's already on it."

"That's enough, Mr Nkwanu," Mr McKlop said, firmly, but a guffaw had already escaped Coach Brown's mouth.

When Caleytown had finished their practice they gathered round their coach.

"Not long now until our first match. We're playing Tewel Primary – but I don't really care about that. All I care about is that you enjoy yourselves today..." Mr McKlop tailed off.

Apart from Janek, no one was listening to him. They were all hypnotised by Royal Road's warm-up drills, which were taking place behind his back.

Balls flew between zigzagging players, who never once made a mistake.

"Oh, wow... They're really good," Jordan said.

"Really, really good," Calum agreed.

Aware that his words weren't going to get

through, Mr McKlop stood up and tossed a football at Janek, the only player who was still looking at him.

"Dodgeball!" he shouted, waking half the squad up from their trance. "Bibs versus tops."

Calum and his teammates stared at their coach, trying to figure out if he was for real.

Janek got straight on board and threw the ball at Ravi. Unsurprisingly, the goalkeeper caught it.

Mr McKlop laughed. "That's a freebie, Janek! Look out tops, bibs have it."

Ravi's eyes widened as he searched for Lewis. He launched the ball at his red-haired friend.

"Ugh." Lewis dived out of the way. "Nae luck, Ravs!"

The rest of the squad finally realised that Mr McKlop wasn't joking.

Leo giggled and sped after the loose ball. He scooped it up, looked for Fraser's orange bib, and launched a mean, curling throw at him.

Fraser squealed and tried to leap out of the way, but was too slow: the ball caught him right on the bum.

"You're out, Fraser," Mr McKlop chuckled.

"Unlucky, Frazzler!" Leo shouted. He hadn't even noticed that Jordan had grabbed the ball and launched it straight at his head.

6

Let the Games Begin

The ball flew towards Leo in the penalty area. He planted his feet and powered a header past Tewel's goalkeeper to put Caleytown 1–0 up.

A couple of camera flashes went off behind the goal, and Leo made sure to celebrate in front of them.

"Great finish, Leo," Mr McKlop cheered from the sideline. Behind him, parents, players, and Scotland Stars staff had filled the stands. The huge arena echoed with their shouts.

For Caleytown, the game of dodgeball had worked. The players had relaxed and were playing with smiles on their faces – apart from Calum.

"Cheer up, Cal," Leo said as they waited for Tewel to restart. "You look even more nervous than our twins."

By 'twins', Leo meant Tewel, their opponents. Lining up for kick off had been like standing in front of a huge mirror. Tewel's right wing looked spookily similar to Leo. Their centre forward had freckles in exactly the same places as Calum and was the same height. And their central defensive duo were mirror images of Janek and Jordan.

The only difference between the teams was that Tewel looked utterly terrified.

I'll cheer up when we win, Calum thought and chased after the ball.

Tewel tried to piece together another attack but it was Caleytown's fans who were soon celebrating again, this time for another brilliant interception by Janek Powolski.

He waved Lewis, Leo and Calum out to the sideline to form a chain – just like they had in Mr Aziz's shop.

"You ready, Cal?" Leo shouted over his shoulder as the ball flew up the pitch from Janek to Lewis, and from Lewis to Leo.

Leo passed it on to Calum, who drifted inside like James Cauldfield often did, and ripped a shot past Tewel's keeper.

2–0. Game over.

Fraser and Leo arrived to sandwich their friend.

"Come on, Cal! Smile for the cameras!" said Leo as more flashes went off behind the goal.

"Yeah, Calum, if you can't be happy now, when can you be?" Fraser joined in.

"When we qualify from this group, alright?" Calum said and jogged back to his own half.

The players stood on the sidelines after the match, skooshing water into their mouths. Their parents smiled and waved from the stands: Calum and Leo's parents were standing together and giving them both a thumbs-up.

At one end of the huge hall, a big screen came to life. Reiss Robertson's face appeared – it must have been almost four metres tall.

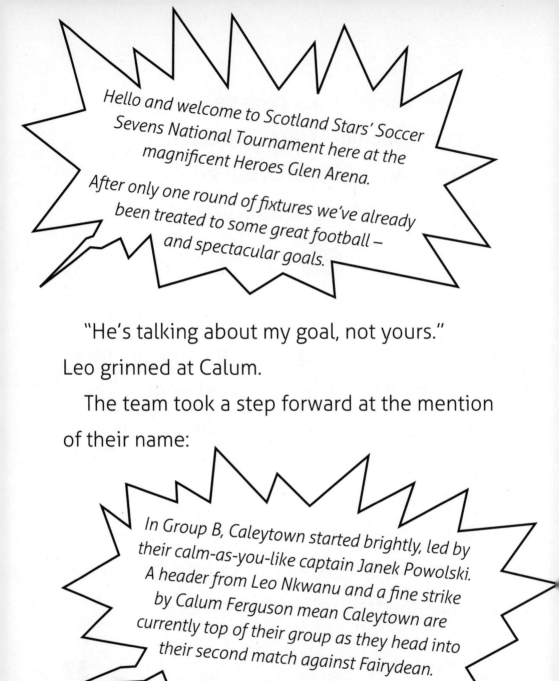

Hello and welcome to Scotland Stars' Soccer Sevens National Tournament here at the magnificent Heroes Glen Arena.

After only one round of fixtures we've already been treated to some great football – and spectacular goals.

"He's talking about my goal, not yours."

Leo grinned at Calum.

The team took a step forward at the mention of their name:

In Group B, Caleytown started brightly, led by their calm-as-you-like captain Janek Powolski. A header from Leo Nkwanu and a fine strike by Calum Ferguson mean Caleytown are currently top of their group as they head into their second match against Fairydean.

Leo nodded his head and patted Calum's back, while Janek took a drink and stared at the screen as if Reiss was talking about someone else.

In Group A, Royal Road scored a whopping total of five times in their opening win against Dundee's Tayport Primary. Striker Adi Adeba notched up a first-half hat trick. Let's watch it again...

"Ah man... I almost forgot about Royal Road," said Leo.

Calum hadn't.

Highlights from Royal Road's opening match filled the screen. They mostly featured their striker Adi Adeba, who seemed to form a fortress around the ball when he had it. In the first clip, he crunched a shot between the keeper's legs with his right foot.

In the next clip he did a step-over with his right to buy a glimpse of the goal, before thumping a cannonball into the top corner with his left.

"What do you think, Janek? Do you see a weakness?" Jordan asked his defensive partner, but Janek put a finger to his lips to shush him.

In the next clip, a super-skilful winger zipped to the byline and hung the ball in the air with a chip. Adeba arrived like a wrecking ball to power a header in off the crossbar and knock two defenders to the ground.

"Wow! A *perfect* hat trick," Fraser whistled.

"Why perfect?" Calum asked.

"A perfect hat trick," Janek intervened, "is a goal with your right foot, another with your left, and a header."

"Anyone else want to play in goal when we face Royal Road?" joked Ravi.

7

Chip, Twist, Vote

Bringing the ball under control with one touch, Calum tried to make space to shoot – but Fairydean's gangly defender had him covered.

He checked his options. Leo was close. But, more surprisingly, defender Janek was steaming forward in support. It was a rare sight.

Calum dummied a pass to Leo, spun and rolled a pass into Janek's path instead.

Fairydean's keeper had no choice but to sprint out to block the shot. Like everyone else in the arena, he expected the big captain to simply thump the ball at goal. He flung himself at Janek's feet.

But Janek fooled everyone with a delicate chip that rose over the keeper... and landed neatly over the line to make it 1–0.

"Yeaa—" Calum's cheer stuck in his throat. He watched in horror as Fairydean's keeper clattered into Janek's standing leg before he could pull it out of harm's way.

"ARGH!" Janek yelled in pain before he even hit the ground.

The sight of Janek lying injured on the ground was the last thing Calum wanted to see.

Sweating with the effort, Janek sat up then tried to stand, but his ankle buckled and he fell back down.

"Stay down, Janek. Let us take a look."

Mr McKlop arrived with Coach Brown to kneel down next to the big defender, who was staring at his ankle like he no longer trusted it. They helped him off the pitch and sent Max on as sub.

Janek nodded to Max as they passed each other. Max was quite a few kilos heavier than his captain, but somehow he seemed to take up less space in defence.

"Come on, Fairies!" Fairydean's central midfielder, and captain, bellowed, before hoofing a pass back to his defence from the restart. "There's still time to win this!"

"*Fairies?*" Leo grinned widely at Calum.

But Calum was in no mood for jokes. He started to drift back instead of forward, until he was closer to his own box than he had been at any point during the tournament so far.

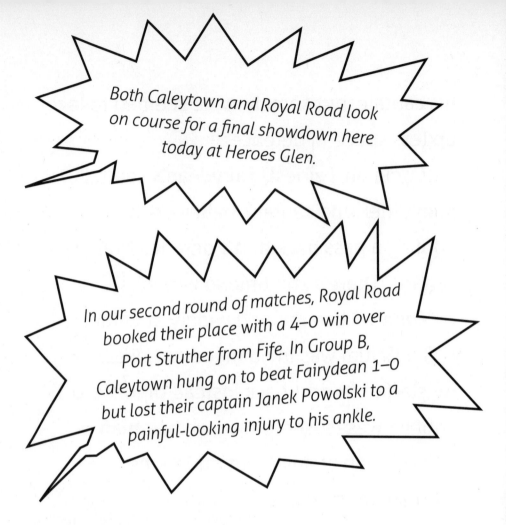

> Both Caleytown and Royal Road look on course for a final showdown here today at Heroes Glen.

> In our second round of matches, Royal Road booked their place with a 4–0 win over Port Struther from Fife. In Group B, Caleytown hung on to beat Fairydean 1–0 but lost their captain Janek Powolski to a painful-looking injury to his ankle.

Reiss Robertson's voice drifted into Caleytown's changing room from the speakers in the corridor. The windowless room had plastic silver walls that were dimpled like goosebumps, and it smelled of feet. Caleytown were waiting for Mr McKlop to return from the first-aid station where Janek had been taken.

"Without Janek, we've no chance," said Calum, slumping down onto the bench. "We've not even got a captain."

Jordan rose to his feet and pointed a thumb at his own chest. "I'll be captain."

"The team should decide who becomes captain, Jordan," said Erika. As the only girl in the tournament,

Erika had her very own changing room, but she had come to theirs for the team meeting.

"Oh yeah?" Lewis rose to stand next to his friend. "Who says?"

Right on time, Mr McKlop appeared at the door. "*I* say, Lewis."

Jordan and Lewis sank back down to the bench.

"I'm afraid it's bad news, gentlemen." Mr McKlop took his glasses off and rubbed his eyes. "Janek's ankle might be broken, so I'm going to have to drive him and his parents to hospital for an X-ray."

"What? Why? Can't his parents or Coach Brown drive him?" Leo blurted out.

"They came by bus, Leo, and the minibus has broken down, remember? More important than that, however, is that as his coach, I am responsible for his injury. Each of my players' welfare is more important than the tournament."

Calum slumped down between Erika and Leo, folding his arms across his chest.

"Look, it breaks my heart to leave you guys like this, but Coach Brown will keep you right." Mr McKlop glanced around the room at his dejected players. "And before I leave, we're going to have a quick vote for your new captain. Please stand up if you want to be considered."

Jordan rose to his feet.

"Yuss," Ravi and Lewis said under their breath.

The rest of the players stared at the ground. Calum certainly didn't want to be captain. For him, playing in the finals was already proving to be too much pressure. Then he felt two hands reach in behind him and shove him off his seat. He stumbled forward onto the floor.

"YES!" Fraser squeaked.

On either side of the gap where Calum had been sitting, Erika and Leo looked around the room pretending nothing had happened.

"Er, I said 'stand', not 'fling yourself onto the floor', but thank you, Calum. Thank you, Jordan. If there are no other candidates then please go outside and wait in the corridor while we vote."

Winning
Isn't Everything

The long, bright corridor outside the changing rooms ran right underneath the main stand. The two captain candidates, Calum and Jordan, stood listening to the muffled cheers and footsteps above their heads.

Calum noticed that Jordan seemed smaller away from his friends, like a toy with some of the stuffing removed.

"I didn't know you wanted to be captain."
Jordan broke the silence.

"Neither did I. Leo and Erika shoved me off
my seat."

A group of players from a team Calum didn't
recognise jogged past them. Their rubber
studs squeaked on the floor. After they'd
disappeared back through the door to the main
arena, Jordan folded his arms and cleared his
throat.

"I think you'd be alright at it," he said, with a
sniff.

"Alright at what?" asked Calum.

"Being captain," Jordan said to the ground.
He glanced sideways. "I don't even want to be

captain – not really. I just know that Dad thinks I should be. With the crowd, my dad and all the scouts watching it's... it's too much."

"I know exactly what you mean." Calum nodded. It felt good to talk about the pressures of the day.

Jordan glanced up and down the corridor. It was completely empty.

"Here." Jordan stuck out his hand to clasp Calum's for a handshake. "Whichever one of us they vote for, let's make a deal that the other one will still support them."

A cheer from the stand above their heads made both boys look up at the ceiling.

"Deal," Calum said and took Jordan's hand.

Jordan immediately let go when the changing-room door swung open. He puffed his chest out as usual and strode back in.

Calum followed.

Inside, the changing room smelled worse than it had before. It really needed a window or two.

"I've counted the votes," said Mr McKlop once Calum and Jordan had sat down. "I want you all to promise to back your new captain while I'm gone. Alright?"

The players all nodded. Calum too. After their honest chat, he'd be happy to support Jordan.

"Ok. It was close but our new captain is... Calum Ferguson."

"What?" Calum felt the room wobble around him.

"YES!" Fraser sprang out of his seat and punched the air.

Calum felt Leo and Erika's hands pat his shoulders. He still couldn't see straight.

Over on the other side of the room, Lewis and Ravi looked to Jordan for how to react.

"Fair dos," Jordan shrugged. He kicked at

some rolled-up tape on the ground. Lewis and Ravi nodded and folded their arms.

"Thanks, Jordan," Mr McKlop said. "Now listen. Calum will be picking the team until I get back, so follow his instructions. Coach Brown will be here in a min—"

"Right y'all, let's stop sittin' around feelin' sorry for ourselves and go get warmed up for our Scapa game!" Coach Brown clapped her hands from the doorway. She handed Mr McKlop his car keys and nodded. "Janek and his parents are all set. Caleytown, follow me to Pitch Two! Hut, hut, hut!"

The changing room filled with the squeaks of astro studs. Just as Calum was leaving,

Mr McKlop tapped him on the shoulder. "Calum, could I have a quick word?"

The corridor outside was busier now. Mr McKlop walked with Calum in the opposite direction to the rest of the team, past bins full of half-empty plastic bottles and rows of lockers.

Caleytown's twins, Tewel Primary, emerged from their changing room and jogged past them. Their eyes were still full of fear – even their coach looked terrified.

"Your team voted well, Mr Ferguson." Mr McKlop put a hand on Calum's shoulder.

"Did they? But I don't like shouting and

telling people what to do."

"Did you ever hear Janek shout in training?" Mr McKlop pushed open double doors to the car park.

"I guess not."

The hot sun hit Calum's face. He had to shield his eyes from the light.

Once they had adjusted to the glare outside, Calum spotted Janek in the passenger seat of Mr McKlop's car, still wearing his captain's armband. He and his parents gave Calum a sad wave.

"You see, Calum, a good captain gains respect from their team by knowing what can make each player stronger. I think you'll be great at that."

Calum stared at the ground.

"And all captains lead by example, Calum, so you'll definitely need to start enjoying yourself out there. Winning means nothing if you didn't enjoy playing in the first place."

Calum could see himself grimacing in the reflection of his teacher's glasses. He tried to relax his face and smile.

"That's more like it!" Mr McKlop smiled back. "If you can keep doing that on the field, you and your teammates will be just fine, win or lose. Off you go to Pitch Two now; you're in charge."

Mr McKlop shook Calum's hand and climbed in behind the wheel of his car. He changed his glasses for shades, started the engine and pulled away.

"The armband!" Calum said to the car as it pulled away. He'd forgotten to ask for it.

Calum sighed, went back through the doors and walked down the cool, dark corridor towards the warm-up area.

Tactics Time

The Astroturf felt different under Calum's feet as he jogged over to join his teammates on Pitch Two. Each step seemed to take longer than before.

The team was standing in a huddle by the side of the pitch with Coach Brown.

"Calum!" Fraser shouted.

Everyone turned round. Calum felt more pressure with each new set of eyes on him. He cleared his throat and spoke in the deepest voice he could muster. "So what do we know about Scapa?"

"Only that they're super fit and beat their opponents by chasing *everyone* down," Leo said. He had his now-tattered programme with him.

"You want my advice?" Erika asked.

"Do we have a choice?" Leo grinned.

"Whatever, Leo," Erika huffed, but Calum really wanted to hear what she had to say. He nodded for her to go on.

"We should make them run until they can run no more." Erika got more animated with each word. "Turn their biggest strength into a weakness."

Calum noticed Coach Brown nodding proudly at her daughter's words.

A quiff moved through the Caleytown huddle like a shark's fin until Ravi appeared in front of Calum. "But if we pass too much we'll eventually get caught out. We should go for goals instead."

"Yeah, Ravs is right. Let's score on them," Lewis chimed in.

The whole Caleytown team turned back to look at Calum while he made up his mind. In his imagination, everyone in the arena turned to stare too.

He wished someone else could make the decision for him.

Just then, a small yet strong hand gripped his upper arm. He looked down to see Erika wrapping black tape around it.

"It's not an armband, but it'll have to do, captain." Erika grinned at him.

The tape tightened around Calum's bicep. It felt good to have it there.

Calum took a deep breath. "Erika's right. We don't need to score loads of goals to go through to the final: all we need is a draw. We're going to pass them to death."

Ravi and Lewis groaned and shook their heads. They looked to Jordan for support but he ignored them.

"Time to go through for the match, team. Calum, would you like to make any changes to the line-up?" asked Coach Brown.

Calum stared at her for a moment before speaking. "I guess so. Max is still on for Janek." Calum turned to his P5 friend. "Fraser, do you mind being a sub? I want to bring you on full of energy when they're knackered."

"Aye, aye, captain." Fraser saluted before sprinting on the spot.

Coach Brown nodded her approval.

"That means Ryan will be our right wingback from the start."

The wiry Ryan nodded and pulled his bib off. He and Max shared a nervous look.

TEAM FORMATION:

Ravi (goal keeper)

Jordan (defence)   Max (defence)

Ryan (right wingback)   Lewis (midfield)   Leo (left wing)

Calum (striker, C)

SUBS: ERIKA, EWAN, FRASER

Pass

The Scapa Primary boys bounded onto the pitch like seven red deer. They looked more comfortable running than standing still.

"They look pretty fit," Leo thought out loud.

As the teams got into position for kick off, Calum had an overwhelming desire to be in his back garden dribbling the ball around with his dog, Leighton. He smoothed the ends of the black tape out on his arm and looked around the team.

"Come on Caleytown, let's go!" he forced himself to shout as the ref blew his whistle for kick off.

One touch,
　　　　two touches,
　　　　　　pass.

One touch,
　　　　two touches,
　　　　　　pass.

The ball created crazy patterns across the pitch as Leo passed to Lewis, who passed to Jordan, who passed to Max, who passed to Ryan, who passed to Calum, who passed it back to Leo.

"It's a shame Mr McKlop is missing this," Leo shouted. "I'll bet this is the kind of football he sees in his dreams!"

Calum was too uptight to respond. *I hope this works*, he thought.

But after a good five minutes of non-stop running, Scapa began to hone in on the weaker passers in Caleytown's ranks.

"Ryan – inside," Lewis shouted as the defender got the ball.

Scapa's midfielder heard Lewis's shout too and cut out that option.

Ryan was jittery – and surrounded. In a panic he lumped the ball back to Ravi.

"My ball!" Scapa's striker shouted.

He intercepted the pass-back and prodded it through Ravi's legs.

1–0 to Scapa.

The small number of Orkney fans who'd travelled to Heroes Glen went crazy in the stands.

Ravi snatched the ball out of the net and glared at Calum. "What now, Captain Fantastic?"

"It's ok," Calum croaked, convincing no one. Not even himself.

Caleytown safely passed their way to half-time without conceding any more goals.

The players in yellow formed a huddle around Calum, waiting for him to say something. He clapped and opened his mouth... but no words came out.

After an uncomfortable silence, Calum's teammates wandered away to get a drink, leaving him to fiddle with the tape on his arm.

He picked away at it until he felt a sudden torrent of water spray into his face.

"Wha... what was that for?" Calum wiped his eyes to see a grinning Leo, water bottle in hand. Erika was laughing next to him.

"I was just trying to wash that stupid, mopey look off your face," Leo said.

"What?" Calum still didn't understand why having water sprayed in his face was necessary.

"Try not to worry so much. Come on, let's get back to passing the legs off these..." Leo looked at something written in pen on his hand, "Orcadians."

"Orcadians? Wait, why have you written that on your hand?"

"My mum taught me the word," Leo said. "It's the word for someone from Orkney."

Calum stared at him like his was mad.

"I just like it, alright?"

The ref blew his whistle to summon both teams back onto the pitch.

"You'd better hope your strategy starts to work soon, Calum," Lewis mumbled as he ran past.

The passing continued after the break. Lewis to Calum, Calum to Leo, Leo back to Jordan, Jordan to Max, Max back to Ravi, Ravi out to Lewis, and so on.

Still Scapa raced after every pass.

"Jordan! Play it wide," Leo shouted from the wing.

But Jordan got his bearings wrong and passed it straight to a Scapa player. Their opponents swarmed forward.

Outnumbered, Jordan and Max did their best, but Scapa passed it round them and Ravi to make it 2–0.

Caleytown's chances of making the final were getting smaller by the minute.

Calum looked over at Jordan, who appeared to be holding back tears. Calum knew he must be thinking about the scouts, and his dad, watching his mistake.

In the stands, Caleytown's fans sat quietly while the Orcadians were doing a conga around their two rows of seats.

It's all my fault, Calum thought as he traipsed back for the restart.

"CALUM!"

He looked at the double doors under the huge screen and felt the urge to run away.

"CALUM!"

Wait, someone was shouting at him.

"CALUM!"

He turned towards the voice. It was Erika.

"Look!" She pointed at Scapa from the sideline.

Scapa Primary all had their hands on their knees and were sucking in air. They had barely celebrated their goal. They were shattered.

"It's working, Calum!" Erika shouted. "Attack, attack, ATTACK!"

Frazzle Them

The sight of Fraser bursting onto the pitch, like a freshly wound-up toy, caused a few of the Scapa players to visibly wince.

"Show them what you've got, Frazzler!" Leo shouted across from the other wing.

Fraser stood on his toes and saluted. His big eyes shone.

"Let's see some of

that Frazzamattazz!" Coach Brown called from the sideline.

Within a minute, the P5 winger had Caleytown's fans up and out of their seats with a lightening-quick dribble to the Scapa box. The gasping Scapa boys just couldn't stay with him.

Running forward, full of new energy, Calum responded to Fraser's every movement. He waited for the winger to make the cutback, darted ahead of a gasping defender and poked home Caleytown's first goal against the Orcadians.

Goal by Calum Ferguson for Caleytown, 2–1. Remember folks, Caleytown will need to score only one more time to equalise and book their place in today's final.

Fraser sprinted across and launched himself onto Calum's back.

He really does weigh nothing at all, thought Calum.

"Great finish, Cal!" Fraser shrieked in his ear.

"Don't celebrate yet, Fraser. We still have work to do."

Fraser slid off Calum's back like a burst balloon.

"Don't listen to Mr Serious here," Leo joined in. "That was some dribble, Frazz."

Leo's words stung, but Calum was too terrified of losing to care. It would all be his fault if they went out now.

00:33 ... 00:32 ... 00:31 ...

Thirty seconds on the clock for this Group B finale. Who will go on to play Group A's winners for the tournament cup?

It was clear that Scapa were there for the taking. Only there wasn't much time left to take them.

Scapa panted forward, but Lewis barged his tired marker off the ball like he was pushing back a curtain. He played the ball diagonally to Leo.

00:15... 00:14... 00:13...

Leo dribbled straight at Scapa's defence.
Their centre-back came forward for the tackle.
Left-footed Leo nodded his afro one way but
jinked the other, opening up some space for a
shot.

00:09... 00:08... 00:07...

With his weaker right foot, he curled an
arcing shot round the keeper and...

CLUNK!

...the ball came off the post and...

$$00{:}03\ldots\quad 00{:}02\ldots\quad 00{:}01\ldots$$

INTO THE NET!

That's 2–2 folks. What drama!
Caleytown get the point they need
with the last kick of the game! Incredible!

This time, Calum did celebrate. He rode a wave of relief towards the big yellow huddle that was bouncing up and down around Leo.

"I didn't know you had a right foot."
Calum hugged his friend.

"I only use it for special occasions,"
Leo laughed into Calum's armpit.

Calum looked over to the sideline to see
Erika and her mum celebrating. He caught
Erika's eye and gave her a thumbs-up.

Caleytown were in the final.

Sneaky Peek

Our next game is the final Group A clash between Royal Road and Forth Hill. The winners will play Caleytown for this year's trophy.

Reiss Robertson's voice filled the building. In the main hall, his face would be filling the screen too, only Leo and Calum couldn't see it.

They had snuck off to grab some food from their changing room.

"Hey, sorry about what I said on the pitch, but what's the point in playing if you don't enjoy it, Mr Serious?"

Calum ducked the question by rushing to push open what he thought was their changing-room door.

But it wasn't their changing room at all.

Inside, Royal Road were lit up by the glow from a projector screen. On it were animated displays of their tactics for their final group game, and a video showing Leo's goal from the match they had *just* played.

Like robots, Royal Road's players all turned

at once to look at Calum and Leo.

"Hi, sorry, hi," Calum stuttered as he backed out over the threshold.

"You can't be in here." One of the coaches nearest the door stood up and closed it in their faces.

Calum and Leo stood with their noses an inch from the grey door.

"Well... that was weird," Leo said.

Sitting up in the stand watching Royal Road play Forth Hill, Calum was beginning to feel a little sorry for them. Royal Road were under so much pressure.

On the sideline, their three coaches stood like toads on a lily pad. Every so often they would shout out the same thing in three different ways:

Move it wide, Adi!

Out to the wing, Adeba!

ADI. WINGER. NOW!

But the constant criticism didn't seem to affect the players too much. Up front, striker Adi Adeba was squat and strong, and his right foot was like the hammer of Thor.

Calum and Leo winced as he smashed the ball at goal. The striker had hardly noticed the Forth Hill defender who literally bounced off him in the process.

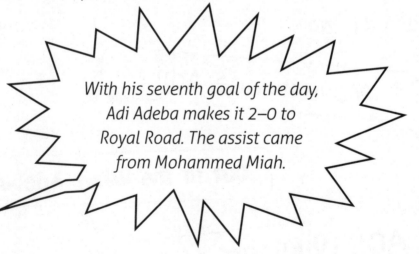

With his seventh goal of the day, Adi Adeba makes it 2–0 to Royal Road. The assist came from Mohammed Miah.

That was the other thing. It wasn't just Adi Adeba that Caleytown would have to be wary of in the final. Out on the wing, Mohammed Miah was a huge threat too. When he dribbled, his feet created a speed-blur around the ball, making it impossible to tackle him without committing a foul.

Royal Road's captain, Noah Hampton, floated a pass to Mohammed Miah. The winger kept the ball in the air with his knee and, without raising his head, hit a long airborne pass to Adi Adeba. The striker jumped, took the ball on his chest and, in one movement, volleyed it past Forth Hill's keeper.

3–0.

The ball hadn't touched the ground since leaving Noah Hampton's boot. The Scotland manager Graeme Fletcher was standing, clapping slowly and shaking his head in disbelief.

Calum looked along the stand at his teammates. Their mouths were hanging open. It wasn't a pretty sight.

"What do we do, Cal?" Leo asked. "Watching this until we need to change our underwear isn't healthy."

Calum played with the tape still stuck to his arm. "I've got an idea but, I dunno, maybe it's stupid."

Erika leaned forward from the seat behind him. "Come on, Cal. Just say it."

Calum cleared his throat. "Does anyone fancy a game of doubles on Pitch Two?!"

Just Because Doubles

Out on the quieter and brighter Pitch Two, Caleytown soon found that a game of doubles at Heroes Glen was just like a game of doubles at school or in the park. Everyone was enjoying the distraction and the goals were flying in.

"Don't look now, team, but we've got company," Coach Brown said between her teeth.

Calum pretended to tie his lace so he could take a look. He spotted a Royal Road coach filming their game on his tablet.

Leo had clocked him too. "Hmm... I've think I've got an idea," he whispered to Calum.

Leo won the ball from Ravi's kick out. Calum ran to face him but Leo started doing step-over after step-over. He even held each arm in the air like he was doing some kind of Scottish country dance.

The Royal Road scout frowned and looked up from his screen.

Calum counted twenty step-overs before his friend finally tripped over his own feet and fell to the ground.

Fraser ran up to help his doubles partner out and keep possession. Leo grinned up at him and nodded over at the Royal Road coach.

A smile unfolded across the young winger's face. He got what Leo was up to.

Fraser took control of the ball from Leo, jinked past Calum then took a massive dive when Lewis tried to tackle him.

Everyone else, including Coach Brown, began to work out what Leo had started.

Everyone except Jordan, who took a pass from Lewis and tried his hardest to beat Ravi in goals.

Much too early, Ravi dived at Jordan's shot like an injured cat and punched the ball into his own net.

"Yeeeessss!" Jordan celebrated. He looked round at his teammates. "Wait, what are youse lot sniggering at? Stop it!"

Leo and Fraser were trying so hard not to laugh out loud that they could barely breathe.

The ball came to Calum from Ravi's dodgy clearance. Calum blazed the ball so high over the bar that it made a big 'Clunk' sound when it hit the metal wall. Lewis planted him on his bum with a pretend rugby tackle.

They both lay on the ground, no longer able to hide their laughter, while Coach Brown jumped up and down like a cheerleader.

Over on the sideline, the Royal Road coach had seen enough. He tutted, clicked his heels, and stormed off.

Jordan was close to a full-blown tantrum. "*What* are you all laughing at?"

He didn't get to find out, because Reiss Robertson's voice boomed over the tannoy:

The tournament final will begin in twenty minutes. Please will Royal Road and Caleytown report to the main pitch.

The Grand Finale

On the pitch, each player was introduced to James Cauldfield and the Scotland manager Graeme Fletcher in turn. Reiss Robertson read their names out on the loudspeaker so the crowd could hear too.

And, finally, on Caleytown's right wing, Fraser McDonald!

117

Another huge cheer echoed round the vast arena.

"Two wingers? That's quite an attacking line-up you've got there, Calum." James Cauldfield smiled down, his head framed by the bright lights on the roof. "Whatever happens, enjoy yourself. These matches don't come along often."

"He's right, for once," Graeme Fletcher joined in. The expression on his face made it seem like he was in constant pain. "Three things every footballer needs to be good at: control, passing and enjoying each game they play."

"Thank you, sir." Calum felt himself salute. *Agh. Who salutes? Except Frazzler.*

"May the best team win," said Graeme Fletcher. He went to join Reiss Robertson in a pitch-side studio for the Scotland Stars report, but James Cauldfield hung back and leaned to whisper something only Calum would hear:

"I'll be supporting Caleytown all the way, of course."

Filled with pride, Calum wished James

Cauldfield was still playing for Caleytown Primary today. They would need all the help they could get against Royal Road.

"You know, Cal, it's not too late to put Ryan back on for Fraser." Lewis had appeared at Calum's side. "We need more defenders on the pitch."

Instead of answering, Calum scanned the crowd for his parents. He found them still standing next to Leo's mum and dad. They were all smiling down at the team.

"Oi, Budgie! Leave him be. Let's just get on with it," a nervous-looking Jordan called to Lewis.

PEEEeeeeeeEEEP!

The referee sounded his whistle. "Captains, please."

Up close, Noah Hampton's Royal Road strip was blindingly white. Calum felt like he was standing in front of some sort of god. Compared to their opponents' outfits, Caleytown's strips looked a bit worse for wear.

Hampton won the toss. "We'll kick off, referee." He spoke to the referee like he was staff.

"We'll... uh... we'll stick with this end," Calum mumbled so quietly that the referee had to cup his hand round his ear to hear him.

Heroes Glen fell silent. Calum thought about shouting something to his teammates but it didn't feel right.

The referee blew a short, sharp whistle and Royal Road kicked off. The crowd started to roar.

Calum ran forward. He was so busy thinking about everything that could go wrong, he wasn't even sure who was controlling his legs.

Get it to Mohammed!

Play it wide to Miah!

NOAH. WING IT. NOW!

The three coaches shouted at Royal Road's
captain, who followed instructions and played
it out to Mohammed Miah.

"Why do you have black tape on your arm?
Did someone die?" Hampton scoffed at Calum
as they watched Miah dribble forward.

Calum blushed at the peeling tape wrapped
round his arm.

Deep in Caleytown's half, Leo tried to get at the ball, but Miah whizzed past him, his feet a blur.

Jordan rushed in to block Miah as he cut into Caleytown's box, but his clumsy tackle sent the Royal Road winger flying a metre in the air.

The referee blew his whistle and pointed to the spot. "Penalty!"

"Excellent!" Noah Hampton pushed Calum out of the way and ran forward to get to the ball.

Let Adi take it, Noah!

It's Adeba's penalty, Hampton!

NOAH. LEAVE IT. NOW!

Hampton swept his hair to the side and left the ball on the ground for the striker. "I'm going to ask Daddy to have a word with those idiots," he muttered as he jogged back towards Calum. "They shouldn't be speaking to me like that."

In goal, Ravi's quiff was dead still. He clapped his gloves together and waited for Adeba's strike.

"Come on Ravi, come on Ravi, come on Ravi," Calum whispered from the halfway line.

Adeba took a decent run-up and belted the ball straight down the middle.

His shot travelled so fast, Ravi didn't even have time to dive. The ball smacked off his face and into the net. 1–0.

Caleytown's keeper fell backwards with his hands over his nose. It was bleeding by the time he hit the ground.

To his credit, Adeba was already standing over Ravi with a concerned look on his face. Calum sprinted over to help.

"Did I zave id?" a groggy Ravi asked.

"Don't worry about that, honey." Coach Brown had arrived with some water and a sponge. She turned to the sideline and shouted, "Erika, you're on!"

15

When All is Lost, Start Having Fun

The incident with Ravi put Adi Adeba off his game. But by half-time, Mohammed Miah and his teammates had still managed to pepper Caleytown's goal with shots. Only Erika, the post and the crossbar had kept the score at 1–0.

Calum hadn't enjoyed a second of it. Not only was he terrified of losing another goal, or four, he felt embarrassed that Royal Road were outplaying them in front of *everyone.*

Strangely, their opponent's coaches didn't seem to think that was the case.

> Not good enough, Royal Road, jog it in!

> Get over here now, Royal Road. This is a shambles!

> ROYALS. HERE. NOW.

The players in white tramped off the pitch with their heads down.

"This is too much," Lewis said, his face as red as his hair. "We cannae hold them. We need more defenders!"

"He's wight!" Ravi said from under the towel he held to his nose. "Do zomefing, Cawum."

Calum felt the tape peeling and flapping on his arm. He ripped it off in frustration.

"I don't CARE any more! Do what you wan—"

"Can I have a quick word, captain?" Calum felt a large hand on his shoulder. He spun round mid-meltdown to see Mr McKlop's smiling face.

"Mr McKlop! You came back!"

"Course I came back." Mr McKlop gave the team a wave before steering Calum to the side. "Coach Brown texted me to say you'd led the team to the final."

"To get shown up in front of everyone," Calum mumbled.

Mr McKlop's smile faded. "Is that what you think?"

Calum felt tears pricking his eyes as he nodded. He wanted to take his yellow boots off and never put them back on again.

"Look!" Mr McKlop turned Calum round and pointed at his mum and dad, classmates and teachers in the stand. "All these people are so proud of you already. Do you know why?"

Calum shook his head. He wiped his eyes with the back of his hand.

"Because you've given your all to get to this final," Mr McKlop said. "You needn't be so afraid of losing, Calum, because in everyone's eyes – including mine – you've already won. Anything that happens now is a bonus."

Calum looked up at his parents in the stands. His dad gave him a thumbs-up.

"I'm only going to say it one more time, Calum: you've got to enjoy yourself when you play football. Otherwise, what's the point?"

Calum smiled for the first time since they'd pranked Royal Road's coach. It felt good. "How's Janek?"

"Good news: his ankle's not broken. Just a bad sprain. In fact, that reminds me. He wanted me to give you this." Mr McKlop took the captain's armband out of his pocket and wrapped it tightly round Calum's arm. "Now, go and help the team enjoy this final. They look like they need your help."

Calum walked back to his teammates, grinning from ear to ear.

"What's with the clown face, Cal?" Lewis huffed. "Can't you see the scoreboard?"

Calum twisted his armband so the 'C' faced outwards. "Do you want to start having some fun, Caleytown?"

Leo started bouncing on the spot with Fraser. "Always, captain!"

The Rainbow Flick

PEEEEEEEEEP!

Leo and Calum powered straight forward from the kick off, catching Royal Road flat-footed.

Calum shimmied past Adi Adeba and squared it to Leo. Mohammed Miah stretched out his leg to tackle, but Leo nutmegged him and powered on up the pitch.

CLOSE THE SPACE!

THERE'S TOO MUCH SPACE!

ROYALS. SPAAAACE. ARGGHHH!

Calum got a return pass from Leo with his back to goal, but the dazzling defender Noah Hampton arrived behind him. Without thinking, Calum flicked the ball up and started juggling the ball with his feet to buy Leo and Fraser some time.

"*What* are you doing?" Hampton and Lewis spoke at the same time.

"Calum, Calum!" Fraser yelled through a laugh.

Calum controlled the ball, spun round an angry Noah and rolled a pass to Fraser.

"Flick it up, Frazzler!" Calum called.

The crowd gasped as Fraser lifted the ball into the air with a beautiful rainbow flick.

It rose straight up and fell perfectly into Calum's path. He waited until the ball was just below knee height before unleashing a fierce volley at goal.

Royal Road's keeper dived but it was too late – Caleytown were now level with them.

1–1.

Calum leaped up and punched the air. On the sideline he caught James Cauldfield doing the same thing.

Leo jumped on Calum's back, and Fraser on Leo's. All three of them tumbled to the ground laughing.

Calum looked up. A knot of red hair blocked out the lights on the arena roof.

"What are you lot playing at?" Lewis asked, but he was holding out his hand. "Let us join in too!"

Royal Road weren't used to their opponents making a game of it. They stood looking at each other as if they'd just met.

At the restart, it was obvious Noah Hampton disapproved of Caleytown's new fun-loving attitude. "Who said you could do keepy-uppies? Don't you realise that this is a tournament final?"

When the answer popped into Calum's mind, it felt like a key turning in a lock. "What can I say, Noah, we just love playing football."

A ripple of surprise rolled over Hampton's handsome face.

But then, everything Caleytown had done in the second half had taken Royal Road by surprise. The yellow-and-whites hadn't managed to score again, but their playfulness had the crowd on their feet many times.

With the final whistle only a minute away, Calum stood and soaked up the atmosphere. Caleytown's parents, friends, and even James Cauldfield broke into song.

"Caley, Caley, Caleytown, Caley, Caley, Caleytown, Caley Caley, Caleytown, Our team goes marching ON, ON, ON!"

00:03 ...
00:02 ...
00:01 ...

The clock wound down.

PEEE-PEEE-PEEEP!

The referee blew for full-time.

With the scores level, we move to golden goal. The first team to score shall win today's Scotland Stars Soccer Sevens trophy.

But we believe that every team here today is already a winner. Let's hear it for them all!

Reiss Robertson drew a huge cheer from the fans.

On the pitch, Calum felt his second-half swagger ebb away.

"First to score wins?" he asked Leo. "Even if one goes in off Hampton's bum?"

"Yeah, Cal, but we've got bums too," Leo said. "We just need to make sure we get ours in front of theirs!"

Flying Geese

The cheering and singing in the stands faded away to a murmur. Everyone waited in hushed excitement for extra time and the drama of a golden goal.

Caleytown formed a huddle around Mr McKlop. He took his glasses off, squatted down and looked at every one of them in turn.

"Jordan, Erika, Ravi, Max, Ewan, Lewis, Fraser, Leo, Calum, Ryan and *Janek*, wherever he is. I wanted to tell you that, no matter what

happens next, I'll never forget those names."

The ref blew his whistle on the halfway line. Calum barely noticed. All he could hear was his teammates breathing in with pride.

"You're the best team I've ever coached and I'm going to miss you a *lot* next year."

Coach Brown sniffed behind Calum and blew her nose.

"Now, go and enjoy yourselves one last time for me!" Mr McKlop shouted.

The noise of Heroes Glen ramped up again and flooded back into Calum's ears. He sprinted to the halfway line.

Time for a golden goal.

Mohammed Miah moved down the sideline, his eyes fixed to the ground, his feet once again a blur. He looked like he was going to dribble round every single one of them and then straight off the pitch.

Time to pass, Mohammed!

Where's the pass, Miah?

MOHAMMED. PASS. NOW!

Watching the winger's feet slow down was like watching a film return to normal speed after fast-forwarding. He cut the ball across the green turf to a midfielder whose first-time pass found Adi Adeba.

The striker drew his foot back, the ball at his feet like a rock in a catapult, and fired.

Only, he hadn't seen Jordan McPride arriving at his side. Caleytown's defender stretched out a long leg and blocked the shot.

"Yass, McPride!" Leo shouted, but the danger wasn't over. The ball had spun out to Miah once more.

Leo sprinted back towards goal.

Get that cross in, Mohammed!

Now the cross, Miah!!!

MOHAMMED. CROSS. NOW!

But Miah wasn't listening this time. Instead of following orders, he dribbled straight for Erika.

Janek's replacement, Max, tried to halt his progress but was scared to tackle in case

he gave away a penalty. Miah drifted past him until there was nobody but Erika to beat.

She sprinted out and dived at Miah's feet. But the winger was ready for it – he chipped the ball over her body...

With camera flashes lighting the way, Royal Road's golden goal was sailing towards the net...

But right then, Leo flew through the air!

He strained his neck muscles and nodded the ball over the bar.

"'Mon the geese!"

Leo's dad's voice boomed out before anyone else in the crowd had a chance to draw breath.

Jordan hauled Leo to his feet to scream in his face, in a good way.

Calum smiled as he watched the rest of the team surrounding his friend. Even Erika gave him a quick hug before getting her defence organised for the corner.

"Right, that's it," Noah Hampton said within earshot of Calum. "I want my triple bonus."

"What... what do you mean?" Calum blurted out.

"My stepmother is giving me a bonus for each goal. It's triple the money for a goal in the final," Noah called over his shoulder.

Calum was speechless. He'd never heard of

players getting bonuses for primary-school football.

He watched Miah place the ball at the corner and raise both hands in the air. And he watched the name 'Hampton', in gold lettering, sprint into his team's box.

The corner swung through the air straight towards Hampton. He leapt up, drew his head back...

"Erika's ball," Caleytown's keeper yelled as, like a superhero, she flew through the air with her arms outstretched and punched the cross away with two fists.

The Golden Goal

Erika's clearance landed right at Calum's feet on the halfway line. Knowing Erika as Calum did, he thought she'd probably meant it to land there.

He turned, fully expecting a challenge, but all six of Royal Road's players were still in Caleytown's box from the corner.

There was nobody between Calum and the Royal Road goalkeeper.

"Go, Calum, go!" Calum heard his mum shout.

The situation felt familiar. Calum suddenly

remembered their litter-picking exercise in training. All he had to do was take the ball to the net. It was that simple.

He took one step,

then two steps,

then three.

"Come on, Calum! This is it!" Leo shouted.

Nearing the box, Calum thought about his first ever breaktime game with his new friends at Caleytown. The game where he'd worn his clunky school shoes.

From that first day at his new school to this moment, had been some journey. And now, there were only a few more steps to take.

The Royal Road keeper's worried brown eyes came into view.

Dive, keeper!

Get at the ball, goalie!

KEEPER. DIVE. NOW!

Under pressure from his coaches, Royal Road's goalkeeper flung himself at Caleytown's gifted number nine.

Calum floated over the keeper's diving body with the ball on his toes and landed on the other side.

The goal sat open in front of him, like a new chapter.

Calum took a final step towards it and smashed the ball into the back of the net.

Players, parents, friends, let's hear a big Heroes Glen roar for our new Scotland Stars Soccer Sevens champions:
Caleytown Primary!

A huge cheer went up. The Caleytown squad, flanked by the Scotland manager Graeme Fletcher on one side and James Cauldfield on the other, stood with fifty phones and cameras pointed at their faces.

"I could get used to this," Leo said, gripping on to his gold medal.

Calum squirted water in his face.

"Hey, what the hell was that for?"

"I'm just trying to wash that daft grin off your face," Calum laughed.

The players broke apart and drifted off to see their parents, carers, brothers and sisters, uncles and aunties, and grannies and granddads.

"Hey, Caleytown, got a message for Captain

Powolski?" Mr McKlop held a phone screen up with Janek's face looking calmly out at them.

"Wish you were here, Janek!" Leo shouted. "We saved you a medal!"

Janek did his best to smile.

"Do you see now, Captain Ferguson?" Mr McKlop said. "Football's a lot easier when you're enjoying yourself."

"You're right... gaffer." Calum gave his teacher a cheeky smile.

"Seeing as you scored the golden goal, I'll let you off with that," Mr McKlop laughed.

"Now, Calum, Leo, go and speak to your parents. I think there's someone over there who wants a word with you both."

Mr McKlop walked off, with Janek still on the phone, to speak to Lewis, Ravi and Jordan. They all put their arms around each other to sing the Caleytown song to Mr McKlop's phone screen.

"Hey, lads." Calum and Leo bumped into James Cauldfield on the way to see their

parents. For a moment, they were both stunned into silence.

"It's James Cauldfield," Leo whispered.

"Are you guys not used to my face by now?" James Cauldfield laughed. "Anyway, do you see that man chatting to your parents? The one wearing the gold-and-black tie."

They strained to catch a glimpse of a smartly dressed man with slicked-back hair.

"I want to introduce you to King's Park Athletic's head youth scout."

"Uh... uh... what... who... what?" Leo and Calum stuttered together.

Reliving the Glory

On Monday morning, the sky was cloudy and the streets were a mix of greys and browns. As Calum walked to school with Erika and Leo, it didn't feel like Caleytown's P6s had just achieved the impossible task of winning the Scotland Stars National Tournament. In fact, it felt as if nothing much had changed at all.

It was only when they got closer to school that they saw the banners hanging from the fences.

At the school gates, Calum saw his classmates patting Lewis and Ravi on the back. Jordan was there too, his collar popped, telling tales from the tournament.

"There's our star striker!" Erika's friend Sally yelled. She ran over and gave Calum a massive hug. "Well done, Cal!"

Calum didn't quite know what to do.

He wasn't much of a hugger, unless someone had just scored a goal. "Erm, thanks, Sally?"

Inside the school it was the same – teachers and pupils all nodded and congratulated Leo and Calum as they walked to class. The P7 boys stayed quiet, of course. They hadn't made it to the tournament the year before.

The two friends ducked into their classroom, ready to high-five Mr McKlop, but he was back in teacher mode.

"Morning, gentlemen – quieten down. This is a classroom, not a football pitch," he said with a wink.

Leo and Calum glanced at each other and smiled.

At break, the whole squad sat around on the sun-warmed Astroturf, talking about their favourite P6 football moments. Janek had a protective shield on his ankle and Ravi's nose was still a little bruised.

"Maybe Mr McKlop knew what he was doing after all when he made us do that crazy assault course," Ravi laughed.

"And the litter picking..." added Fraser.

Ryan groaned at the memory. "Remember the sheep on the pitch when we played Fieldling? Maybe that was a test too."

"Yeah! I think Ravi's still got some sheep poo in his hair!" Jordan pointed at Ravi's quiff.

The goalkeeper meticulously checked his hair.

"Do you think Mr McKlop ever found out about our pranks at Muckleton?" Calum asked, remembering when they'd risked forfeiting the tournament to tie wool all over their rival's goalposts.

"I think we might have known about it if he did," Erika said. A satisfied silence fell over the team. The sounds of the other kids shouting and screaming filled the air.

"So when's your big trial at King's Park?" Jordan asked, quietly.

"We don't know yet." Calum shrugged. "They're going to send our parents an email."

Jordan nodded. Janek smiled.

"Caleytown Primary, Scotland Stars champions," said Lewis. "Sounds good, doesn't it?"

"Caley-Caley-Caleytown," Fraser sang quietly.

"...Caley-Caley-Caleytown," Max and Ewan joined in and rose to their feet.

"Caley-Caley-Caleytown," Jordan helped Janek to his feet. Leo, Calum, Erika, Ravi, Ryan and Lewis all stood up. They formed a huddle and started bouncing – apart from Janek, of course.

"Caley-Caley-Caleytown, our team goes marching ON, ON, ON!"

SCOTLAND STARS SOCCER SEVENS NATIONAL FINALS
CALEYTOWN 2 – 1 ROYAL ROAD

REISS ROBERTSON REPORTS

Even Scotland manager Graeme Fletcher was left scratching his ginger head after Caleytown pulled off the mother of all upsets to halt Royal Road in their tracks.

The super-talented favourites had courted controversy after what some called 'unfair investment' from millionaire Proctor Hampton in his son's school team. But, on the day, hard work, team spirit and a love of playing football was enough for Caleytown to wrestle the trophy from their hands.

When Caleytown's keeper went off dazed and confused after taking an Adi Adeba penalty in the face, many would have predicted more goals for the Royal Road striker and his teammates. But Caleytown Girls' Team sub Erika Brown is a talented stopper, and Caleytown are no walkovers.

Emerging with a spring in their step from their half-time team talk from Coach Iain McKlop, they dazzled the crowd with an exuberant goal by Calum Ferguson.

It was Ferguson again who, after a tense deadlock, ran half the length of the field to leap over Royal Road's stopper and thwack the golden goal home.

Scotland Stars has enjoyed watching the rise and rise of this Central Wildcats team of underdogs, or should we say undergeese. For them, and many of their players, the future looks bright.

DANNY SCOTT, a die-hard football fan, works for Scottish Book Trust and is the goalie for Scotland Writers F.C.

ALICE A. MORENTORN is a children's book illustrator and a teacher at Emile Cohl School of Arts in Lyon, France.

 Smash it!

It's easy. You can either kick a ball at a wall and control the rebound or simply kick or throw the ball in the air and control it. The key is to do it over and over again until controlling the ball becomes automatic.

Remember – and this is important – it's not enough just to stop the ball. Practise until you are able to control a pass with one touch and shoot or pass with the next. It might take a while, but it's worth the effort.

 Scorefest!

A great game to play in pairs

Taking turns in goal, you each get 5 shots from far out, 5 from the edge of the box, and 3 penalties. (If you're not on a proper pitch, decide the distances yourself.)

Scoring:

A goal from far out = 5 points

A goal from the edge of the box = 3 points

A penalty goal = 1 point

Good luck!

MR AZIZ'S FOOTBALL JOKES

GRAB THE WHISTLE

If you were the referee, would you make the right call?

1. A player kicks the ball so hard it bursts. What do you do?
a) Duck and run for cover
b) Grab another football and restart the match with a drop ball
c) Call full-time

2. A goalkeeper kicks the ball out, it bounces over the opposing keeper and lands in the net. What do you do?

a) Award the goal

b) Ask the keeper to take it again

c) Make sure the opposing keeper is awake

3. A player's boot comes off during his run-up to a penalty. He still shoots and scores. What should you do?
a) Cover your nose so your can't smell his sock
b) Ask the player to put their boot back on and retake the penalty
c) Award the goal

Answers: 1b, 2a, 3c